CUENTO
DE LUZ

To Laia: live your dreams.
- Susanna Isern -

To my parents, who always helped me to achieve my dreams; including the dream of flying.
- Silvia Álvarez -

Bear Wants to Fly
Text © 2016 Susanna Isern
Illustrations © 2016 Silvia Álvarez
This edition © 2016 Cuento de Luz SL
Calle Claveles, 10 | Urb. Monteclaro | Pozuelo de Alarcón | 28223 | Madrid | Spain
www.cuentodeluz.com
Title in Spanish: Oso quiere volar
English translation by Jon Brokenbrow
ISBN: 978-84-16147-66-3
Printed by Shanghai Chenxi Printing Co., Ltd. March 2016, print number 1566-1

FSC
www.fsc.org
MIX
Paper from
responsible sources
FSC® C007923

Bear Wants to
FLY

Susanna Isern * Silvia Álvarez

It was late, late at night, deep in the dark forest. Bear was standing next to the lake, with a glum expression on his face. Owl spread out her beautiful white wings, and silently glided down towards him.

"What's up, Bear?" she asked.

"I need you to help me out, Owl," said Bear. "I guess it might sound a bit crazy, but my dream is to be able to fly."

"**B**ear wants to fly!"

All of the animals were amazed by the news, and decided to meet up immediately.

"A flying bear?" croaked Frog. "That's impossible!"

"Maybe not, if we all work together," said Ant.

Wolf nodded and said, "I think we should try."

"Hooray!" hooted Owl. "Let's share the plan with everyone!"

Eagle, the highest flyer in the forest, was happy to offer some advice. "A light body and feathered wings is the first thing Bear will need. It is essential to know how to move and to have the right posture. But above all, you have to trust in yourself."

The animals set to work.

As the sun began to rise over the forest, Raccoon scurried to Bear's den.

"Wake up, sleepyhead! It's time to start your new exercise program. I'm going to get you in tip-top shape for flying!" Also you'll have to eat less honey and more leaves, fruit and fish.

Meanwhile, the other animals gathered colorful feathers of all kinds to make a beautiful pair of wings for Bear.

On the other side of the hill, Bear and Raccoon reached the seashore. A friendly penguin was waiting for them in the water.

"Are you ready to learn how to fly, Bear?" he asked.

Bear was surprised. "But I thought penguins couldn't fly!"

"We are the only birds who can fly through the sea. Jump in! Trust me!"

Finally, the animals had gathered enough feathers—hundreds and thousands of them—to make a pair of wings for Bear.

The woodpecker and the termites carved a light frame out of wood. The finches and the spiders, who are great weavers, bound the frame together using strands of grass.

One by one, each feather was carefully attached to the frame with honey and tree sap. The animals worked hard from dawn to dusk, over the weeks and months.

One afternoon, when Frog teaching Bear to make great big leaps, they saw an ant who had fallen into the water, and was clinging to a fragile leaf.

Bear, Frog, and the other animals watched nervously. The poor little ant was drifting away, and the leaf was gradually sinking into the water.

"Come on, Bear! Quickly! Our sister's in danger," said the ants.

"Me?" stammered Bear, worriedly. "But it's such a long way down to the water!"

"It's now or never. You can do it! Remember everything I've taught you," said Frog, his voice full of encouragement.

Bear closed his eyes and took a very deep breath. Then, with his heart pounding in his chest, he jumped into the water. When he finally rose to the surface, he reached out and rescued the little ant.

Back on dry land, the butterflies flapped their wings to dry off the ant. Then Squirrel carried her away to a safe place.

Everyone hugged Bear for being so brave. He hadn't just saved the ant; he'd learned how to leap, even if he was afraid.

Spring arrived in the forest, and Bear was finally seeing the results of all his hard work.

He looked much slimmer. He'd practiced so much that now he could fly through the sea just like a penguin, and could even jump into the river doing somersaults through the air.

Everything was nearly ready, including the wings!

When the animals had finally attached the very last feather, they set off to find Bear. Moving through the trees of the forest, the giant wings looked as if they were flying all on their own, like magic.

Bear saw them in the distance, and rubbed his eyes to make sure he wasn't seeing things. As they drew closer, he began to feel very excited.

At last, it was time for Bear to fly! All the other animals climbed to the top of a hill. Bear put on his wings.

"You're much lighter now!" said Raccoon.

"You must swim just like a penguin!" said his little black and white friend.

"Don't be afraid to jump!" said Frog.

"These wings are strong enough to keep you up in the air. They will help you land softly too," said Wolf.

Bear took a deep, deep breath, closed his eyes, unfurled his wings, and jumped.

Eagle, Owl, and all of the other birds flew alongside Bear to keep him company.

Bear flapped his wings, but he started to lose height. Eagle flew beneath him, and flapped his wings at just the right speed until Bear climbed back into the air. Gradually Bear stopped wobbling around, and one by one, the birds left him to fly on his own.

Up on the hill, the other animals looked on with a mixture of joy and satisfaction. When they worked together, they could move mountains. Nothing was impossible.

As the sun began to set, Bear finally learned to fly like a bird. From high up in the sky, everything seemed smaller: unreachable dreams, impossible challenges, even his problems.

The bright, friendly moon rose high in the sky, as the animals on the hill felt their hearts fill with pride. Bear soared through the clouds as his tears of happiness were carried away by the wind.